The Little Drummer Boy

Contributing writer
Carolyn Quattrocki

Cover illustration
Linda Graves

Illustrations
Susan Spellman

Louis Weber, C.E.O.
Publications International, Ltd.
7373 North Cicero Avenue
Lincolnwood, Illinois 60646

Manufactured in U.S.A.

8 7 6 5 4 3 2 1

ISBN: 0-7853-1363-X

PUBLICATIONS INTERNATIONAL, LTD.
Candy Cane Books is a trademark of Publications International, Ltd.

P9-DSZ-773

A long time ago near the town of Bethlehem lived a boy. His family was very poor.

The little boy had one thing that made his life happy. He had a drum. Years before, when his grandfather was a young boy, a group of traveling musicians had come to Bethlehem. They gave his grandfather the drum.

When the boy was old enough, he learned to play *pa-rum pum pum pum.* Now the drum belonged to him.

The little boy loved his drum more than anything in the world. He played it every day all around his village.

The other children would follow behind him, marching and singing as he played.

The people in the village began to call him the Little Drummer Boy. They smiled when they heard him playing and singing:

Pa-rum pum pum pum.

At the same time in a town called Nazareth, there lived a young woman named Mary. One day an angel told Mary that she would have a son.

Mary and her husband, Joseph, were planning a trip to the town of Bethlehem. Caesar Augustus, the ruler of the land, had ordered all the people to go to the town where they were born so that the tax collectors could count them.

Mary was expecting her baby to come very soon.

When Mary and Joseph finally arrived in Bethlehem, it was crowded with all the people who had come to be counted. Joseph looked and looked for a place to spend the night, but no one had room for them.

Finally one innkeeper said, "I have no room inside, but there is a stable behind the inn where you could stay overnight."

Mary and Joseph were so tired that they were happy to have any place to spend the night.

During the night a baby boy was born. Mary named the boy Jesus. She made a bed for him by putting him in a manger.

That night some shepherds were out in the fields. An angel appeared and told them about Jesus. The angel told the shepherds to go to Bethlehem.

Then many more angels appeared and started to sing, "Peace on earth and good will to all." When the angels left, the shepherds hurried to town to see the baby Jesus.

Everyone was talking about baby Jesus and wanted to bring him gifts. The Little Drummer Boy wanted to see Jesus, too, but he was too poor to bring a gift. What present could he give?

That night the Little Drummer Boy saw a most wonderful sight. In front of him were three kings carrying many beautiful gifts.

The Little Drummer Boy listened as he followed them. "There is the star we have been following," said one king. "See, it is pointing us toward the stable up ahead."

The three kings followed the star to the stable where the baby Jesus lay in a manger.

"I am Melchior," said the first king. "I have brought a gift of gold for Jesus." The second said, "My name is Gaspar. I have brought a rare perfume known as frankincense." "And I am Balthazar," said the third. "I, too, have brought a valuable perfume called myrrh."

The three kings laid their gifts before the manger.

The Little Drummer Boy was sad because he had no gift to give. But he started playing and singing:

Come, they told me,
  pa-rum pum pum pum,
Our newborn King to see,
  pa-rum pum pum pum.
Our finest gifts to bring,
  pa-rum pum pum pum,
To lay before the King,
  pa-rum pum pum pum,
So to honor Him,
  pa-rum pum pum pum,
When we come.

Baby Jesus,

  pa-rum pum pum pum,

I am a poor boy, too,

  pa-rum pum pum pum.

I have no gift to bring,

  pa-rum pum pum pum,

That's fit to give a king,

  pa-rum pum pum pum.

Shall I play for you,

  pa-rum pum pum pum,

On my drum?

Baby Jesus smiled at the boy. Everyone in the stable knew that the boy was giving the best gift of all— the gift of love.